PET

Oxford University Press, Walton Street, Oxford OX2 6DP

Oxford New York Toronto
Delhi Bombay Calcutta Madras Karachi
Kuala Lumpur Singapore Hong Kong Tokyo
Nairobi Dar es Salaam Cape Town
Melbourne Auckland Madrid

and associated companies in
Berlin Ibadan

Oxford is a trade mark of Oxford University Press

Copyright © Val Biro 1995
First published 1995

A CIP catalogue record for this book is available
from the British Library

ISBN 0 19 279956 8 (hardback)
ISBN 0 19 272200 X (paperback)

Printed in Hong Kong

Lazy Jack

Retold and illustrated by
Val Biro

Oxford University Press

Once upon a time there was a poor old woman who
lived in a little cottage. She made some money by
knitting, and she knitted busily all day long.

She had a son called Jack. He was so lazy that he sat by the fire from morning to night and never did a stroke of work. So people called him Lazy Jack.

Time came when his mother could stand this laziness
no longer.

'Jack,' she told him one Monday, 'if you don't begin
to work for your porridge now, I will turn you out to
get your living as best you can!'

This made Jack wake up, and off he went that very day to work for a farmer.

When he finished, the farmer paid him a pound.

Jack clutched it in his fist,
but on his way home he slipped
on a bridge and dropped the
pound in the brook.

'You stupid boy,' said his mother.
'You should have put it in your pocket.'

On Tuesday, Lazy Jack went off to work in the dairy. The cowman paid him with a jug of milk.

Jack remembered what his mother had said, so he put the jug in his pocket.

But as he climbed over a stile, he spilled all the milk.

'You silly-billy,' said his mother.
'You should have carried it
on your head.'

On Wednesday, Lazy Jack went off to work at the cheese shop. The cheese lady paid him with a big cream cheese.

Jack remembered what his mother had said, so he put it on his head.

But long before he reached home, the cheese melted and ran down all over his face.

'You dunderhead,' said his mother.

'You should have carried it in your hands.'

On Thursday, Lazy Jack worked at
the cattery. The woman there paid
him with a large tomcat.

Jack remembered what his
mother had said, so he carried it
in his hands.

But the cat scratched him
so much that Jack had to
let it go.

'You nitwit,' said his mother.
'You should have tied it to a string
and pulled it behind you.'

On Friday, Lazy Jack worked for the butcher, who
paid him with a fine ham. Jack remembered what
his mother had said, so he tied the ham to a string.
But by the time he had dragged it home,
only the bone was left.

His mother had lost all patience by then.

'You nincompoop,' she cried. 'You should have carried it on your shoulder!'

On Saturday, Lazy Jack worked at the stables, and
he worked so well that he was paid with a donkey.
Jack remembered what his mother had said, so he
tried to lift the donkey up. But it was very heavy.

At last he succeeded, and began to stagger home
with the donkey on his shoulder.

Now, along that road there lived a rich man with his daughter, who had never spoken a word in her life. She had never laughed, either, and the doctors said that she would not speak until somebody managed to make her laugh.

The girl was sitting sadly by the window now,
looking out, when . . .

. . . she saw Lazy Jack
struggling along with the
donkey on his shoulder,
and the poor animal
kicking his four legs in
the air and hee-hawing
for all he was worth.

It was the funniest sight she had ever seen, and the beautiful girl burst into such a peal of laughter that she was cured instantly.

Her father was overjoyed and rushed out of the house.

'Drop that donkey,' he told Jack, 'and come in to meet my daughter. If she likes you, you can marry her.'

She liked him all right, so they got married on Sunday.
The whole village was there to see them drive from the
church in a cart, which was pulled by Jack's donkey.

Now they live in a fine house,
and Jack makes his beautiful
wife laugh all the time.

Traditional Tales